David Bedford was born in Devon, in the south-west of England in 1969.

David wasn't always a writer. First he was a football player. He played for two teams: Appleton FC and Sankey Rangers. Although these weren't the worst teams in the league, they never won anything!

After school, David went to university and became a scientist. His first job was in America, where he worked on discovering new antibiotics.

David has always loved to read and decided to start writing stories himself. After a while, he left his job as a scientist and began writing full time. His novels and picture books have been translated into many languages around the world.

David lives with his wife and two children in Norfolk, England.

www.davidbedford.co.uk

For Kate
DB

Little Hare Books
8/21 Mary Street, Surry Hills
NSW 2010 AUSTRALIA

www.littleharebooks.com

Text copyright © David Bedford 2006
Illustrations copyright © Keith Brumpton 2006

First published in 2006
Reprinted in 2007
Reprinted in 2010

A CiP catalogue record for this book is available
from the National Library of Australia. (*Australia*)

A CIP catalogue record for this book is available
from the British Library. (*UK*)

ISBN 978 1 921049 34 7

Cover design by Xou Creative (www.xou.com.au)
Set in 13.5/21 Giovanni by Asset Typesetting Pty Ltd
Additional typesetting by Clinton Ellicott
Printed through Polskabooks
Printed at Rzeszow Zaklady Graficzne, Rzeszow, Poland,
January 2010

7 6 5 4 3

the Team #6

MASTERS OF SOCCER

David Bedford

Illustrated by
Keith Brumpton

LITTLE HARE
www.littleharebooks.com

Chapter 1

"*What* did she say?" said Harvey.

It was Monday afternoon assembly, and Harvey had just watched four girls do a dance called *Sleeping Beauty*, which had sent him into a comfortable doze. Now Mrs Pinto, the Headmistress, was talking, but Harvey was yawning so much he couldn't hear her.

"After School Clubs," Darren replied, shaking his head. "It's an experiment — we have to join a club and meet every afternoon this week, starting today."

"School after school?" said Harvey in disbelief. "What about The Team?"

"Looks like football training is off," Darren said moodily.

Mrs Pinto, who was small and bean-shaped and had a high, singsong voice, began to read from a list. "The topics available to students are as follows," she said, clearing her throat. "Kitchen Dynamics. Fabric Awareness. Frontier Exploration."

Harvey heard Rekha whisper nearby, "I think she means Cooking, Dressmaking and Science."

Darren pulled an ugly face to show what he thought of them.

"And last but not least," sang Mrs Pinto, "Sporting Development."

"Huh?" said Darren, looking hopeful but unsure.

"Sports," said Rekha, and Darren shouted "Yes!"

Mrs Pinto peered around the hall before continuing. "On their way out, each student must sign up for their preferred A.S.C."

"After School Club," translated Rekha.

"If a club becomes full," said Mrs Pinto, "please sign up for your second choice. Then proceed to the assigned meeting place. Clubs will begin immediately."

Harvey and Darren scrambled to their feet at the same time. There was no point in hanging about, Harvey knew. They needed to get their names down, and fast.

Darren was the first to line up in front of their teacher, Mr Spottiwoode, who had "Sporting Development" written on a sign hanging around his neck.

"We're doing sport," said Darren and Harvey together, grinning.

Mrs Pinto spoke from behind them. "I'll take these two, Mr S."

Harvey and Darren spun around.

"Follow," said Mrs Pinto, and she headed off at a brisk pace.

Harvey and Darren looked at each other. Harvey shrugged. "We must have done something wrong," he said. "She's not taking an After School Club, is she?"

"Come along, lads!" came Mrs Pinto's call. "Never be late for an important date!"

"I've got a bad feeling about this," whispered Harvey as they waited outside Mrs Pinto's office. Their headmistress had disappeared inside without a word, and it sounded like she was moving chairs and tables about.

Just then, Harvey saw the girls who'd performed *Sleeping Beauty* dance along the long corridor towards them, talking excitedly.

"What now?" said Darren suspiciously, but before anyone could answer, Mrs Pinto opened her door wide.

"In you go!" she chimed, and the girls tiptoed after her.

Harvey and Darren stood side by side in the doorway, peering in. The dancing girls had lined up along one wall, standing with their arms in the air and one leg sticking out. Mrs Pinto was sitting at her desk, which was pushed tight against the wall, leaving a large space in the centre of the room.

"Step up!" said their headmistress, and Harvey and Darren drifted in reluctantly.

Without thinking, Harvey let go of the door, and it swung shut behind him with a worrying *snip*!

"Welcome," Mrs Pinto declared, "to Ballet Extravaganza!"

Darren made a strangled noise. "Nyeear!"

"Pardon?" said Mrs Pinto.

"I think he means …" began Harvey, but he couldn't go on. His legs felt weak, and he began to sway. He felt Darren's hand clasp his. It wasn't holding hands, thought Harvey. They were just holding each other up.

"Well, never mind," said Mrs Pinto. "As I was saying, this is Ballet Extravaganza, or B.E., as we shall call it."

Harvey's hand was being crushed. He could feel Darren trembling.

"I bet not a single person in this school knows that before I trained to be a teacher, I was —" she smiled, "a ballerina!"

The girls erupted into shrieks. "Oh, Mrs Pinto!" said one of them.

Harvey and Darren began to edge backwards. Please, door, don't be locked, Harvey thought.

"I have waited for years to use my ballet skills to train a troupe of my own."

Harvey's elbow touched the door. Darren was nearest to the handle. They began to turn around slowly, careful not to draw attention to themselves.

"What I needed was a 'corps de ballet', a group of dancers — and that, ladies, is you."

Harvey heard the girls whimper with pleasure. Darren silently turned the door handle.

"I have also invited a Dance Master to choreograph a special dance for us," said Mrs Pinto. "That special person will be arriving tomorrow."

Darren gave the door handle a mighty tug. Nothing happened.

Harvey put his lips to Darren's ear and said shakily, "Yank the handle *up* to unlock. You have to —"

"And, most important of all," came Mrs Pinto's voice, "I had to find two strong, capable boys."

There was an ominous silence. Harvey and Darren twisted around to face their headmistress.

"Please, Mrs Pinto," begged Harvey. "We don't know anything about ballet."

"Which is perfect!" cried Mrs Pinto. "You are the empty page upon which our dance shall be written!"

"But we can't dance," pleaded Harvey.

"We've got blisters!" said Darren wildly.

"No need to worry," Mrs Pinto soothed. "Today we're just doing the dressing-up bit. That's mostly for the ladies — you two only get to wear these boring old things."

What she handed to them was red and stretchy, and looked to Harvey like a swimsuit.

"Er, you've given us the girls' ones," he pointed out.

Mrs Pinto took the outfits back, and held them up. "No, no," she said. "They have your names on them."

It was true. Harvey saw that each swimsuit had a name tag sewn on to it. They were for Harvey Boots and Darren Riley.

"Leotards aren't easy to get on first try," said Mrs Pinto. "So take your time. You may change in here."

She opened the door to her storeroom, handed Harvey and Darren their leotards, and waited patiently as they shuffled inside.

Mrs Pinto switched on the light, and closed the door.

Darren was shaking all over with fear.

Harvey felt his legs buckle, and he collapsed to the floor.

"You've got five more minutes, lads!" called Mrs Pinto. "Then we'll all see how lovely you look!"

Chapter 2

"Got to … get out," Darren said. It sounded like his jaw was frozen.

Harvey looked high and low. There were no windows, just a small grille high up near the ceiling, but it was far too small for anything bigger than a cat to squeeze through.

Darren began clawing towards it with both hands, his legs trying to climb the smoothly painted wall.

"It's no good," Harvey said. "There's no way out."

Darren's head whipped around; he spotted a cupboard, and threw himself at it, wrenching open the doors.

"One minute more!" called Mrs Pinto.

The cupboard was filled with books, which Darren scooped out frantically.

"Ten more seconds!"

"There's no point hiding," said Harvey, trying to calm Darren down. He'd never seen anyone panic like this.

Darren pressed himself into the cupboard space just as Harvey grabbed the doorknob, which had begun to rotate. He couldn't stop it moving.

"Five, four, three, two — *ta-da!*" Mrs Pinto pulled open the door so forcefully Harvey was propelled into the office outside. The girls tittered.

Mrs Pinto pursed her lips as she looked first at Harvey, and then at Darren squashed in the cupboard.

"Oh, silly lads!" she said, tutting. "I suppose you might as well keep your school uniforms on for our first few lessons, until you overcome your shyness."

A hot feeling of relief rose from Harvey's toes to his head, making him feel as light as a feather.

Darren emerged, red-faced, but Harvey could tell he was back in control.

Mrs Pinto raised her leg into a kick. The girls copied her. Harvey and Darren watched.

"We're waiting, lads," said Mrs Pinto.

Harvey lifted one leg. Darren lifted his foot.

"Now like this," said their headmistress, raising her arms above her head to make an oval shape.

The girls did the same. So did Harvey, wobbling on one leg. Darren put his hands up as if he was tipping a shot over the crossbar.

"Good, good," said Mrs Pinto, who seemed pleased with them, and Harvey felt his spirits lift. What they were doing wasn't the nightmare he thought it would be — not yet, anyway.

Mrs Pinto checked her watch. "Our time is up, alas. But we shall meet again tomorrow."

Darren grabbed Harvey by the elbow as he marched past. "Out of here," Harvey heard him mumble.

"Just one more thing!" said Mrs Pinto as they reached the door. "B.E. is a *secret* club. Anyone who spills the beans will be answerable to ME."

She unlocked the door for them, and stood aside to let them out.

"As if we'd *tell* anyone!" Darren said angrily, under his breath.

They had trudged halfway along the corridor before Mrs Pinto called, "Repeat the exercises before bed each evening. Hard work really does pay off, you know. And you will need all the practice you can get for the performance."

Harvey and Darren stopped so suddenly they might have run into an invisible brick wall.

"A performance!" said one of the girls.

"Do you mean it?" said another excitedly.

Mrs Pinto was beaming with pleasure. "Yes, my dears, it is quite true. We will be performing in front of the whole school on Friday morning!"

With a muffled cry, Darren sprinted away. Harvey, faint with terror, did the same, and didn't stop running until he'd reached the safety of Baker Street.

There was no way he and Darren would dance in front of the whole school. Never.

But right now he couldn't think of any way for them to get out of it.

Chapter 3

Harvey's house was at the top of Baker Street. Next door, there was a tower shaped like a rocket about to take off. Professor Gertie, who was an inventor, lived there with her greatest invention, the football-playing robot Mark 1.

The best thing about having an inventor living next door, Harvey decided when he woke up on Tuesday morning, was that inventors knew how to fix problems. Fixing problems was what they did best.

Before leaving for school, Harvey knocked loudly on the tower door. There was a furious clattering coming from inside. It sounded to Harvey like an elephant typing on a keyboard.

There was no answer.

Harvey banged louder. The clattering stopped.

"Hey!" called Harvey. "I know you're in there!"

There was a long silence.

"Professor!" called Harvey. "I —"

Professor Gertie's face appeared at an open window, and Harvey hurriedly told her about Ballet Extravaganza. "And then on Friday we have to perform in front of everyone," he finished. "Though of course, we won't."

"Why not?" said Professor Gertie curtly.

Harvey goggled at her, amazed. Perhaps she didn't understand. "It's ... *ballet*!" he said. "And we're *boys*."

"Boys do ballet," said Professor Gertie. "I don't know what all the fuss is about."

"But —!" said Harvey.

Professor Gertie frowned and blinked. "The thing is," she began, beckoning Harvey closer as if she was about to tell him a secret. "I'm not supposed to, but ..." Suddenly, Professor Gertie shook herself, and her voice became sharper. "No, I can't. You'll just have to go with the flow, Harvey. All I can say is, hard work really does pay off. Got that?"

Harvey opened his mouth, but couldn't speak. Those were exactly the words Mrs Pinto had used!

"Later, alligator," said Professor Gertie, with a wave goodbye as she slammed the window shut.

"Later," breathed Harvey, totally confused. Professor Gertie was behaving strangely — very strangely. And as Harvey headed off to school, he was beginning to wonder why.

When Harvey arrived in the classroom Darren was sitting at his desk looking like he didn't have a care in the world.

"We're sorted," Darren said, giving Harvey the thumbs up.

"You mean we don't have to go back to …" Harvey lowered his voice as he sat next to Darren, "B.E.?"

"Oh, we'll be prancing about all right," said Darren lightly. "There's no way Pinto will let us out of it — not if she can help it."

"Then how are we sorted?" said Harvey.

"We take Friday off." Darren leaned back and rubbed his hands together, satisfied.

Harvey thought about it. It sounded like a good idea — if they could get away with it, that was.

"How can we?" he asked curiously.

"No problem," said Darren. "I only have to tell my mum I've got a sniffle and she makes me go back to bed. I had the most days off in the whole school last year, remember."

Harvey nodded, recalling how proud Darren had been when he'd found out.

"What about me?" Harvey said.

"You stay over at my place," said Darren. "The next morning, we both say we're going to puke, and we both go back to bed. My mum will be even more worried about you. There's no way she'll send you to school."

Harvey smiled. It sounded easy — too easy, almost.

"The only bad part is that we have to hop about in Pinto's room for three more afternoons. But at least we're only doing it in front of the Sleeping Beauties, and they're not allowed to tell anyone. That's the main thing, Harvey. *Nobody will know what we're doing.*"

The classroom was filling up, and Darren lowered his voice.

"We should try to look like we're enjoying it," he said. "That way, Pinto won't suspect anything, and it will be a big surprise for her when we're not there at the very *silly* B.E. performance."

"B.E.?" Paul Pepper was standing over them. "What's that?" he demanded. "And why weren't you two at Sporting Development?"

He raised his voice so that everyone could hear. "Sounds to me like Harvey and Darren are doing Fabric Awareness! Or is 'B.E.' even more of a joke?" Paul Pepper cackled, and to Harvey's dismay he saw Rekha look at them over her shoulder, mouthing "B.E." to herself and frowning.

Harvey's heart began to race. He was sure Rekha was about to guess what "B.E." meant, but in the end she just gave him an odd look before turning away.

Darren was definitely right. The main thing was that nobody would ever know what they were doing. If they did, he and Darren would never live it down.

Chapter 4

Darren strode along beside Mrs Pinto, with Harvey and the Sleeping Beauties behind. There was nobody about — the other After School Clubs were being held in a different building.

"I hope we haven't got too far to go," Darren said airily. "Because I don't want us to waste time when we could be, you know, wagging our knees about and stuff like that."

Mrs Pinto took a sharp left into a classroom. Darren hesitated. It was pitch-black inside.

Click!

Light flooded the almost-empty room. Harvey, joining Darren, saw right away why it had been so dark. Large lengths of brown paper had been taped over the windows.

"It won't be a surprise performance if everyone already knows what we've been up to," said Mrs Pinto with a wink.

"Perfect for keeping our secret," Harvey said to Darren.

Harvey began to relax when Mrs Pinto asked them to line up for the first exercise without even once mentioning leotards.

And then he heard heavy, clumping boots coming along the hallway.

"Hide!" said Darren, his good humour gone. "We can't be seen here!"

They crouched behind a pile of chairs.

The footsteps grew louder, then, right outside the room, they stopped. There was a *whirr*, a creak, and a low hum as Mark 1, the Football Machine, entered the room.

"Everyone, please welcome our Dance Master!" chimed Mrs Pinto.

"Hi-ho," the robot said in his strange, mechanical voice.

"Is Mark 1 going to teach us ballet?" said Harvey incredulously as he and Darren emerged from their hiding place.

"Yes indeed!" said Mrs Pinto. "He comes highly recommended."

"By who?" Harvey asked bluntly, sure that he'd already guessed the answer.

"Oh, you know," said Mrs Pinto lightly. "He was revealed to me by a rather *inventive* new friend of mine."

Harvey had a sinking feeling. There was no doubt about it. Professor Gertie was involved. And knowing her, she'd planned everything from the start. But why? She and Mark 1 were always one hundred percent behind Harvey. What could possibly have turned them against him?

Harvey shook his head to clear it. That couldn't be right. Professor Gertie had never let him down. There had to be some other explanation — though Harvey couldn't imagine a good one.

Suddenly, Mark 1 bent so far over backwards he could place his hands on the floor. Harvey thought he looked like an upside-down, four-legged spider.

"Ouch," said Darren. "That looks painful."

"Nonsense," countered the headmistress. "You'll be doing that yourself by the end of the week. Now, there's just one more thing we need."

With a flourish, she picked up a large plastic shopping bag from behind a piano that stood in one corner, and tipped out the very last thing Harvey expected to see.

It was yellow and fluffy, but there was no mistaking what it was.

"Why have you got a football, Mrs Pinto?" he asked, picking it up.

Mrs Pinto took it from him. "Let's find out, shall we?" She made as if to walk away, then turned suddenly and said, "Heads, Harvey!" Swinging her arm wide, she launched the ball straight at him.

Caught by surprise, Harvey just managed to nudge the ball with his head, directing it back to his headmistress.

"It's really soft!" Harvey said, amazed. It had felt like heading a sponge.

"It's a Squishy Squash — a ball specially invented for indoor use," said Mrs Pinto.

Professor Gertie again, thought Harvey. "Squishy Squash" was just the kind of name she would give to one of her inventions.

"We will use the Squishy Squash so that we don't smash windows or hurt anyone. Darren — catch!" Her arm extended again, this time sending the ball high over their heads.

Darren leapt for it, but the ball slipped through his fingers.

Harvey couldn't help snorting. "Sorry," he said. "But it was a bit butterfingers, wasn't it?"

Darren looked hurt, but their headmistress was beaming. "That's the idea!" she said. "You almost had it. You just need a little more *poise*. A touch of *finesse*."

"A touch of what?" said Darren, perplexed.

"Throw to me," ordered Mrs Pinto.

Darren scooped up the ball and tossed it to her casually. Harvey was sure he had aimed it deliberately wide. Then, to his astonishment, the headmistress plucked the ball from the air with an enormous leap, landing lightly on her toes with the Squishy Squash held between her tiny outstretched hands.

Someone was clapping. Harvey looked towards the girls, but it wasn't them. Nor was it Mark 1, who was sitting cross-legged on the floor, thoughtfully pressing his button.

Darren clapped again, hands above his head. "Awesome save, Mrs Pinto," he said, his eyes wide.

"I don't get it," said Harvey, shaking his head. "Are we doing ballet, or playing football?"

"You will be exploring ball-based skills through the medium of balletic dance," said Mrs Pinto. "Let's begin."

When Harvey headed home that evening he was thoroughly confused. They had been doing B.E., which he was supposed to hate, and yet he felt as if he'd just been in the best football training session ever. Darren had made some incredible leaps to catch the Squishy

Squash, sometimes even managing to land gracefully on one foot. It was perfect practice for The Team's goalkeeper.

Harvey had found he could knock the ball whichever way he wanted it to go with any part of his foot, even the sole, if he used his arms to balance.

Meanwhile, Mark 1 had demonstrated tackle moves to the Sleeping Beauties, who were quick learners, and probably good enough already to try out for The Team.

Harvey's whole body was aching, but that was good. It meant his muscles were working hard. And hard work really did pay off.

Harvey stopped, thinking of Professor Gertie again. He was outside her tower, but all was silent. Cupping his hands around his mouth, he called, "What's going on, Professor?!"

He waited for an answer, but instead he heard a piercing shriek from up the street.

Turning, he saw Rita, his attacking partner on The Team, pedalling her bike towards him, waving and spluttering words so fast he couldn't understand a thing.

She fell off her bike and began limping towards Harvey, holding one of her trainers, which had slipped off.

She was almost breathless with excitement. "COMING!" she gasped. "HERE! PEDRO MANOLO IS COMING HERE!"

Rita sat down on the kerb, took a huge, steadying breath, and told Harvey again what she'd already told him twice.

"Pedro Manolo is coming to your school on Friday."

Harvey's mouth was hanging open. His eyes had glazed over, and he hadn't blinked for some time. Pedro Manolo was the greatest sportsman on the planet. Everyone knew that.

"He's just been named World Soccer Star for the fifth time in a row," said Rita, "and now he's on tour. Are you all right, Harv?"

"Yeah," said Harvey, whose whole body had gone numb.

"There's some kind of show on in the morning," Rita went on. "I don't know what it is, but all my school is coming to see it. Pedro Manolo will be there. Then there's lunch, and after that, a Manolo Soccer Masterclass!"

Rita stood up. "I have to go," she said. "I just wanted to tell you as soon as I found out, because Pedro's your hero, isn't he?"

"Oh yeah," said Harvey.

"Are you really okay?" said Rita, concerned. "You don't look well. Try to get a good night's sleep. You don't want to miss school on Friday."

"I'll be there," said Harvey, trying to sound cheerful.

As he watched Rita cycling away, he realised he had a simple choice. Either he did a ballet dance in a leotard in front of everyone he knew, or he missed the greatest opportunity of his life.

Chapter 5

When Harvey explained about Pedro Manolo's visit, Darren screwed up his face so tightly he looked like a prune that had stayed in the bath too long. He kept on looking like that for at least five long minutes.

"Darren," Harvey urged gently. It was like talking to someone who was sleepwalking — you had to be careful not to wake them up. "Are you all right? The bell's just gone."

They were standing by the school gates, and everyone else had gone into class.

Darren's nose began to twitch. Suddenly, his eyes flew open, and his wrinkles disappeared.

"Any ideas?" said Harvey hopefully.

"I think so," said Darren.

"And …?" prompted Harvey.

"We modify the plan," said Darren, patting his sore cheeks. "First we're sick, and we have to stay home from school. Then, just before lunchtime, we're well again, and we get to see Pedro."

Harvey thought it through. "We miss the performance, but turn up for the masterclass?" He whistled. "You're really good at this stuff," he said, slapping Darren on the back.

Darren shrugged modestly.

A movement caught Harvey's eye. It was Mr Spottiwoode, waving at them from the window. "If it wasn't for After School Clubs, I'd put you in detention!" he threatened.

"Oh no!" Harvey joked to Darren. "We wouldn't want to miss B.E.!"

Throughout the day, Darren outlined the details of his plan to Harvey. "We have to be sure we look ghastly," he explained. "And the best way to do that will be to use all the tricks of the trade."

"Rub flour in our cheeks?" said Harvey.

"Of course," said Darren. "And chew some toothpaste so that we're frothing at the mouth."

"Right," said Harvey. "What about hot water bottles — should I bring my own?"

"I've got one you can use," said Darren. And then he balled his fists and said triumphantly, "Pedro Manolo, here we come!"

Wednesday afternoon's Ballet Extravaganza was more fun than any school lesson Harvey had ever had.

He and Darren had both got over the embarrassment of doing jumps and stretches and twirls in front of the Sleeping Beauties, and they put all their effort into following Mark 1's instructions, while Mrs Pinto accompanied their movements on a piano.

It was going to be a match. Harvey and Darren were on different teams, and Darren

kept saving all of Harvey's shots. Harvey flicked the ball all over the place in slow motion, while Darren leapt about catching it. After a while, Darren missed a shot, and Harvey celebrated his goal by twirling around and around and flinging his arms in the air a lot. Then the Sleeping Beauties came on and chased him, spinning a lot too, until they caught him. Eventually, Harvey broke free, raced to the ball, and launched it at Darren, hitting him in the stomach.

After that Darren and Harvey had to do some running and jumping about before collapsing in a heap, chuckling.

"Excellent!" declared Mrs Pinto, as the robot picked them up. "Cut out the giggly bit and we're there!"

The next day, Thursday, they planned to practise the dance twice more — but that afternoon, things started to go badly wrong.

First, at lunchtime, Harvey spotted Professor Gertie talking with Mrs Pinto in the school kitchen.

"Now we know for sure," he told Darren. "Professor Gertie's involved. I can't believe she's let us down like this."

"But she always does the best for us," said Darren, puzzled.

"Not this time," said Harvey grimly.

Darren shook his head. "Stop worrying, Harvey, or you really will make yourself sick!"

Later, Harvey overheard Rekha pondering the meaning of "B.E." with Paul Pepper. "You know," said Rekha, "I'm sure it's something to do with Mrs Pinto's secret class, the one Harvey Boots is doing. You don't think the 'B' could stand for 'Ballet', do you?"

Harvey arrived at their last After School Club with Mrs Pinto feeling as if he was being watched.

"Calm down!" said Darren. "We have to look casual — you'll make Mrs Pinto suspicious!"

Harvey tried to act normal, but all he could think about was how often the simplest plans could go wrong — especially when Professor Gertie was involved. He couldn't concentrate at all, and he yelped, startled, every time Mrs Pinto shouted at him for making a mistake.

"Mr Boots," she said as the lesson drew to a close, "you must conquer your nerves! And don't worry, it will be all right tomorrow, I'm sure."

Harvey and Darren were leaving when Harvey saw it.

There was a tiny tear in the paper that was blocking out the windows, and through the tear he saw an eye.

Darting across, he peered out just as Rekha and Paul Pepper skidded around the corner.

So that was that. Even without doing the performance, everyone would soon know that Harvey and Darren did ballet.

"It could be worse," said Darren morosely, when Harvey told him on the way to his house. "At least we're not going to prance about in front of them tomorrow. I can't even imagine how embarrassing that would be."

But as Harvey drifted off to sleep that night, he had the terrible feeling that they were about to find out.

Chapter 6

The first part of Darren's plan worked like a dream.

With flour-white cheeks, frothy lips and foreheads heated with hot water bottles, they had staggered into the kitchen while Darren's mum was making breakfast.

"We're not well, Mum," said Darren.

"Oh, you poor dears," said his mum, holding a hand to each of their heads to check their temperatures. "You're both burning up! And you're as white as a pair of sheets."

"Day off," Darren mumbled, letting toothpastey froth dribble down his chin.

"Of course," said Darren's mum, and Harvey felt a flutter of relief in his chest.

"Then again," said Darren's mum, "what would Harvey's parents think if I just left him alone and didn't take proper care of him?"

"W-what are you on about, Mum?" said Darren, his voice wavering. "Why can't we just stay at home with you?"

"Because I'll be at your school all day, helping Professor Gertie. She's responsible for the Big Bash Picnic at lunchtime, didn't you know? And we're all going to sneak in to watch the secret performance Mrs Pinto has been preparing."

"We'll be okay here on our own," insisted Darren urgently, and Harvey could see his face creasing up as he tried to change the plan. "I'll look after Harvey, and he'll look after me."

"No, no, no," said Darren's mum. "That won't do at all! I'm not letting either of you out of my sight. You can both come with me to school."

Harvey's guts did somersaults as he and Darren put on their school uniforms, with Mrs Riley calling for them to hurry.

"What do we do now?" he kept saying. "Darren, she's your mum — think of something!"

Darren was grinding his teeth. "I need more time to work things out. Whatever happens, Harvey, we're not doing the performance, so there's no need to worry ..." But he looked more worried than Harvey had seen him in his life.

"Come on, boys, you're late!" called Darren's mum.

"We're being sick, Mum!" called Darren desperately.

"Oh, tosh!" she replied.

Darren looked horrified. "I don't understand it," he said to Harvey. "She doesn't believe me!"

"Tosh," repeated Harvey heavily. "That's another thing Professor Gertie says. She's behind all this — and I think we're about to find out what she's been up to."

When they finally went downstairs, Darren's mum threw them their coats, then led them outside.

It was a beautiful, sunlit Friday morning. Birds were singing in every tree and there was a cool, refreshing breeze. Harvey realised he would normally have been looking forward to The Team's match tomorrow, but this week he hadn't even given it a single thought.

Darren walked with his hood pulled right

down and Harvey couldn't see his face at all. Mrs Riley had to drag him through the school gates.

With dismay, Harvey saw Mrs Pinto waiting for them in the shadow of the hall where her After School Club would be performing.

We have to persuade her that we're ill, he thought desperately. It's our only chance.

He half closed his eyes and tried to look feverish, when all of a sudden Darren threw back his hood and declared happily, "Mum! We're not poorly anymore — we're cured!"

"No!" yelled Harvey, digging Darren in the ribs, but it was too late.

"The fresh air did it!" said Darren, who still hadn't noticed Mrs Pinto. "We're as fit as fiddles! So you can leave us right here and go do your Big Lunch thing and we'll be okay."

Darren leaned over to Harvey and whispered, "We'll have to keep our heads down, and —"

"My boys!" said Mrs Pinto.

Darren's face turned to wax as Mrs Pinto took them each by the arm and led them into the empty hall. Harvey began to shudder as they arrived backstage.

"We're really very, very shy," Darren said to her tearfully, but Mrs Pinto only ruffled his hair.

"I know, dear," she said. "But the show must go on!"

The crowd came in, and the music began.

The Sleeping Beauties were standing on the far side of the stage, peeping through the curtain and squealing with delight.

Harvey and Darren were on the near side, huddled together and trying to keep out of sight. How Mrs Pinto had got them to change into their leotards, Harvey couldn't remember, but he thought it was probably because they had run out of excuses.

Neither of them could think of anything to say, so they stood in silence.

The Sleeping Beauties lined up, the way they had practised. The piano grew louder, and with a crash of cymbals the curtains were drawn back. The girls began their opening dance.

Harvey heard some laughing, and then what appeared to be a bored silence.

The music changed. Their time was coming.

A door beside them opened. The first thing Harvey noticed was that sunlight was streaming in. It was a way out.

Then he saw Professor Gertie enter, hot and flustered.

"Almost — total — disaster!" she said, panting. "Didn't know you were at Darren's. Looked everywhere. Need to give you — these!"

She threw Harvey and Darren their red Team shirts, white shorts and socks. "Hope you didn't think we'd embarrass you with those *leopards*."

"I think she means leotards," Harvey whispered to Darren as they frantically pulled on their football kit.

It was like his second skin, Harvey thought, and he immediately felt more confident, and braver, as if he had the whole Team beside him.

"Good luck!" said Professor Gertie, standing with her arms folded and beaming at them.

Harvey heard the music change again, getting ready for the part where he and Darren would begin.

Harvey's legs seemed to know the routine and, without thinking, he took a step forward.

"No," Darren hissed, holding him. "Let's run!"

"Okay," said Harvey, but he didn't move.

"Now!" said Darren, grabbing Harvey's elbow.

Harvey stayed where he was. His whole body had been trained, ready to move when the music said it had to.

Darren was goggling at him. "You can't do it," he said, his lower lip quivering. "Harvey — it's *ballet*!"

Harvey's heart was racing. "I know," he said. "It's just — we're good at it, Darren."

It felt like he was talking about The Team playing football, because it was the same thing. They had worked so hard …

"Everyone knows we did Ballet Extravaganza," he told Darren. "This is our chance to show them that it's not as daft as they think."

Darren turned away, and strode to the door just as the music played their cue.

"Now!" Harvey said, as he had when they'd been practising.

He heard Darren's fast footsteps.

"I'm on my own," Harvey thought, his whole body erupting with goose pimples as he leapt gracefully onto the stage in front of his hero Pedro Manolo, and just about every person he knew.

Chapter 7

The bellow of laughter was like a sudden blast of wind. Harvey lost his balance and knocked into Darren's shoulder, which thankfully put him back on course to catch the Squishy Squash that was already flying through the air towards him.

Darren? Harvey's head snapped around.

Darren was there beside him, looking like he was in complete agony as he twirled, arms flicking wide, to the far side of the stage.

The audience seemed to draw in a huge breath, and then the bellow came again. "HA! Ha ha ha ha ha ha ha ha!"

Harvey, who'd dropped the Squishy Squash to his feet, mis-kicked, and the ball flew far to one side of Darren. But with a tremendous leap, The Team's keeper collected the ball in his two outstretched hands, landed effortlessly on one foot, and sent the ball arcing perfectly back to Harvey.

The spectators fell silent.

Harvey shot at Darren again, better this time, and he heard an "Ahh!" from the crowd as Darren jumped straight up to let it fall into his outstretched palm.

To Harvey's astonishment, there was soon applause each time Darren saved, and when the time came for Harvey to score, there was a rumble of "Boo!" from half of the spectators, and a cheer of "Yes!" from the rest.

Harvey twirled about the stage, celebrating his goal. Each time he outmanoeuvred the

Sleeping Beauties who were chasing him, he heard a "Whoa!".

There was a cry of anguish when Harvey finally booted the ball into Darren's stomach, and excited calls as he and Darren did their prancing about before falling to the floor to the sound of thunderous cheers.

Harvey and Darren were in a fit of giggles as the music stopped.

"It was okay!" Harvey said.

"It was incredible!" said Darren.

"*Magnificent*!" came Mrs Pinto's voice.

Harvey saw Pedro Manolo walking towards them, and he and Darren stood up.

"He'll never believe we're really football players," Harvey said sadly. "That's the worst bit of all."

Pedro Manolo held out his hand — and then he did the last thing Harvey could have imagined. He started to twirl, spinning faster and faster until he was a blur. Then he stopped, grinned, and shook Harvey and Darren by the hand, before taking two gold medals from his pocket.

"These two students," he said loudly, "have shown themselves to be both brave and skilful — they are Masters of Soccer!"

He hung a medal around each of their necks as the crowd went wild.

Harvey felt like he was dreaming.

"Gold," said Darren, awestruck, nudging him in the ribs. "Not bronze. Not silver. *Gold.*"

Harvey, who was staring open-mouthed at his hero, saw Professor Gertie skipping up to them. "Oh, Pedro!" she said, giving the greatest-ever sportsman a kiss on the cheek. "Didn't I tell you they could do it?"

"You did, señorita," said Pedro with a nod, as he was led away by Mrs Pinto, who wanted his autograph.

"You knew about everything!" Harvey accused Professor Gertie, his voice furious and happy at the same time. "I bet it was all your idea, wasn't it?"

"Oh, well, you know," said Professor Gertie mildly. "I just couldn't help myself, not after I read Pedro's book. Have you seen it? It's all about how he secretly used ballet training to help him be as good as he is."

"You're kidding," breathed Darren. "Pedro Manolo pranced about?"

"Ever since he was your age," said Professor Gertie, folding her arms with satisfaction.

"But if you'd told us that in the first place …" Darren rolled his eyes in frustration.

"I wanted it to be a wonderful surprise for you," said Professor Gertie innocently.

"It was," said Harvey with a sigh.

The hall was emptying, but The Team were holding back to talk to Darren and Harvey.

"Absolutely," began Matt.

"Totally," added Steffi.

"Brilliant!" finished Rita.

"But hurry up," said Matt. "I think I can smell our Big Bash grub burning."

"That'll be my mum's cooking," admitted Darren.

"Yikes!" Professor Gertie bounded away. "My kebabs!"

The Team sat with Pedro Manolo through lunch, as he explained the message in his new book, *Soccer Extravaganza*.

"My friends," he told them, "there is just one thing I need to tell you. Hard work—"

"Really does pay off," chorused Harvey and Darren. "We know."

"You've read the book already?" said Pedro.

"We know somebody who has," said Harvey, smiling.

Just then Paul Pepper came up with his own team, the Diamonds. "Is everyone going to be shown football ballet now?" he asked, making sure he was first in line.

"My two experienced teachers will show you everything they know," Pedro promised.

"Where are they?" said Paul Pepper, looking around.

Pedro put his hands on Harvey and Darren's shoulders. "Here."

Paul Pepper blinked. "Come on, then," he said, grumpily. "What are you waiting for?"

Harvey saw that Darren was glowing with pride — and knew he was too.

Just then, Mark 1 arrived, carrying a jumble of what looked like girls' swimsuits.

"I spent days clacking away at my old sewing machine," said Professor Gertie busily. "But I should have enough leopards for everyone."

With great pleasure, Harvey held out the first leotard for Paul Pepper.

"We'll start with the dressing-up bit," he said, and it wasn't long before he and Darren had to hold each other up again — only this time it was because they were laughing so much.

Prof
Gertie

Darren   Harvey

Rita   Matt   Steffi   Mark 1